The Glimpses

Penny Vincenzi

A Phoenix Paperback

The Glimpses first published in *New Woman, New Fiction* by Pan in 1990.
Glass Slipper first published in *Good Housekeeping* in 1994.

This edition published in 1996 by Phoenix
a division of Orion Books Ltd
Orion House, 5 Upper St Martin's Lane, London WC2H 9EA

ISBN 1 85799 746 8

Typeset by Deltatype Ltd, Ellesmere Port, Cheshire
Printed in Great Britain by Clays Ltd, St Ives plc

Contents

The Glimpses

James was a very lucky man. He told himself so quite often, and he listened to his mother and his mother-in-law and his wife's best friends (of whom there seemed to be rather a lot) telling him so quite often as well, and he knew he ought to believe it, and in fact he sometimes did, he managed to persuade himself that it was quite true; he would say yes, I am a very lucky man, very lucky indeed, and he would count his blessings again and yet again and congratulate himself upon them.

Since he counted them so extremely frequently, he knew exactly how many there were and the order in which they came: pretty, loving wife; three beautiful children; nice house (in a good area with good schools); good job in insurance, excellent prospects, fair salary; and then he was very healthy, he didn't have ulcers, and he could beat someone a fair bit younger than he was at squash; and he and Anne, as the pretty loving wife was called, had a very active social life, plenty of friends; and yes, he would say, pushing his rose-tinted spectacles more firmly on, yes, I am very lucky, most fortunate, and he would meditate upon his less fortunate friends and relations who had been made redundant or were getting divorced or who did have ulcers, and compare his lot most favourably with theirs.

It wasn't even as if he and Anne had a sterile or even a dull relationship. They talked and discussed a great deal, they were friends as well as lovers, as she liked to say, and in fact said quite often, and it was true of course, and they were lovers still after nine years, and every six days or so, Anne would turn the light out before he had finished reading, unbutton her Laura Ashley nightie and say 'James' in a particular tone of voice, that was an interesting hybrid of question and command. She always assumed he would be ready for her and of course he usually was, although there were times when he could have wished either for a variation in her approach or more sympathy with his own mood.

Anne had done a course in Self Awareness at the Adult Education Centre, and she knew that it was most important that women should take the initiative in sex whenever they so wished, and moreover that the woman had particular desires and needs of her own, as well as recognizing those of her man; and although she didn't actually feel the needs very strongly herself, she nevertheless wanted James to recognize their existence and how important they were, and not to regard their sex life as simply a gratification of his own.

And James knew, from listening to the coarse banter of his colleagues and squash opponents in various pubs and bars, that they would regard this attitude of Anne's as still further manifestation of his great good fortune, for many of them had to work quite hard to be allowed to gratify their desires, and they would have given their next promotion or place on the squash ladder in exchange for a wife who issued sexual invitations on a regular basis, however predictable they might be. And it wasn't even totally predictable really, James supposed; Anne was quite enthusiastic, just unimaginative and afterwards, when she had climbed back into her Laura Ashley nightie and was talking about her day, which was what she liked to do, he would stroke her hair tenderly and reflect on his fondness for her, and wrench his thoughts away from the disorder of desire and the flesh and back into the neat lines of the PTA, the babysitting rota, the children's progress with their reading and recorder playing, and the literary luncheon appreciation group which Anne had formed.

So there he was, very lucky, very lucky indeed. So how was it, he wondered, that so often, indeed with appalling frequency, depression would strike him in the stomach like a physical blow, the rose-tinteds would slither right to the end of his nose and fall off, and he would see his life for what it really was? And what it really was he knew he didn't really want. What he did want was slightly out of focus and very much out of reach; but he also knew that it was the real thing, not a fantasy, and that if it ever did come along, he would recognize it and reach out for it without hesitation.

It shimmered tantalizingly, both in his subconscious and the real world; but occasionally he would catch a fleeting glimpse of it, and it was like suddenly recognizing the beloved only just ahead, just out of reach, and his heart would thud, his knees jellify and he would reach forward, trying desperately to catch hold of it, to detain it before it was lost once more in the crowd.

The Glimpses, the fleeting glances, sometimes took the form of people, but more often they were an environment, an atmostphere, a feeling of being in the right place at almost the right time. And later, when the Glimpses had gone, and he sat eating Anne's cassoulets and crumbles in the warmth and mess of the family dining room, to the accompaniment of tales of the suburban broods, and much interrupted by small pyjamaed figures, his mind would go back and try to analyse the substance of what he had seen. Gradually the formulation became more precise; what he was Glimpsing was beauty, and beauty of a very worldly kind. It was not sunsets or fireglow or the smile on the face of a little child that made him sick with longing (and indeed he had more than enough of all that sort of thing, particularly the smiles on the little faces), it was still, white rooms and sculptured furnishings, reedy music and dia-grammatic paintings. And the people in the Glimpses were beautiful too: witty and sylish, their conversations designed as carefully as their clothes.

And as he began to know what he was finding in the Glimpses and why he liked them so much he was able to look out for them and to see more of them. He took to going to art galleries in his lunch hour, instead of walking in the park; he would wander through smart furniture shops, drinking in the chrome and the marble, so shiny, so perfect, so unsmudged; and as he grew bolder he would go into the most expensive and chic clothes shops and study not only the cuts and colours on view but the people buying and wearing them, all obviously rich and clever and successful and selfish, not a PTA member nor househusband among them. And although he could not afford the pictures or the clothes or the coffee tables, he would occasionally buy a glass or a handkerchief and he would keep them in his wardrobe, or his desk drawer, as talismans, as living proof that there was another world somewhere, whose lifeblood was not Ribena and finger paints, but fine wine and beautiful books, and the air of which was not filled with action songs and arguments, but esoteric melodies and abstract-based discussions.

Once Anne found a pair of cashmere socks in his wardrobe that he had bought from Paul Smith; her indignation and wrath were more in proportion to the discovery of a batch of lurid love letters. 'Really James,' she said, hurling them on the bed, 'how could you, they must have cost a fortune, you know Dominic needs new dungarees, and your season ticket's about to expire, and you waste' – she looked at the ticket, quivering with rage – 'seventeen pounds on a pair of socks. You must be mad, quite, quite mad, whatever is the matter with you, I bought you six pairs in Marks in April, it's not as if you need socks, I mean if it was a tie, I could understand a bit more, at least that would show, but socks, why socks?'

Useless to try to explain, James knew; sitting, head bowed with shame, clutching the socks, symbol of his profligacy and betrayal, he tried to form a coherent sentence about why socks; because they were a luxury, precisely because they didn't show, because they weren't functional, because only he knew that they were there on his feet; expensive, smooth, soft, unmatted from getting in with the nappies, un-stretched from being used as Christmas stockings. That was why socks.

Later that night, in bed, she was remorseful. 'I'm sorry darling I got so cross,' she said. 'Of course if you think you need some socks, then you should buy them. I don't suppose you realized how much more expensive they were. I'll get you some more tomorrow in Marks, I've got to get Emma some tights, and maybe you could change those for a tie or something.'

'No it's all right, I really don't need any,' said James with a sigh, turning over and deliberately choosing not to notice that she was unbuttoning her nightie, even though it wasn't scheduled for another two nights at least. 'I'm sorry too, but anyway, I couldn't change them for a tie, that would cost at least thirty-five pounds. Good night.' And as he lay awake in the dark, he drew some shreds of comfort from the fact that he knew exactly how much ties from Paul Smith cost, and Anne hadn't the faintest idea.

After that he kept all his trophies in the office.

Time passed and the summer holidays (camping in France) came and went as did Hallowe'en (Trick or Treating with the children) and Guy Fawkes (bonfire in their garden this year, with sausages, tomato soup and mulled wine for all the neighbours), and Christmas began to be heard in the distance.

6   Anne made puddings, cakes and sausage rolls endlessly

('for the freezer,' she explained, as if it was some kind of huge, hungry animal), sewed for the nativity play and planned carol singing; James worried about paying for it all, wondered whether his mother would actually come to blows with Anne's this year, and received an invitation to a Christmas party at one of the galleries where he had become something of a regular and had actually bought a couple of prints (hanging rather incongruously on his office wall, alongside his charts on pension schemes and his department's annual holiday rota).

He saw the Glimpses swimming suddenly and triumphantly into focus, accepted promptly, and then spent many hours worrying about what to wear; the socks of course would be ideal and needed an outing, but something more was needed. Nothing he possessed would be remotely suitable; his smartest suit was outmoded all over by inches, his jeans were over-washed and his casuals only just all right for family Sundays. Finally, feeling rather sick, he took his Barclaycard to Simpsons and bought a light wool beige and brown jacket and some beautifully cut, slightly baggy beige trousers, and then feeling even sicker, a pale blue, faintly patterned silk shirt. It all cost him considerably more than the total allowance he gave Anne to clothe all the children for the winter.

Looking at himself in them though, it was worth the sickening guilt. In the mirror stood not the James he knew, solid reliable chap, faithful husband, selfless father, but someone else altogether. Smooth, handsome even, possibly unreliable, probably unfaithful and certainly selfish; a person in fact from the Glimpses.

He gazed and gazed, enraptured with himself, like an adolescent girl going to a party; then finally, and reluctantly, having taken the clothes off but with some of his new selfishness and style still hung about him, he went to Russell & Bromley and bought a pair of hugely expensive, soft leather loafers. He had thought his brogues would possibly do, but they stood, a sorry piece of sacrilege, beneath the trousers, betraying his homely roots; and besides, he felt he owed it to the socks to cover them with class.

Where to keep it all though? His small pen of an office was clearly unsafe, all he had was a coat hook behind the door, and home was hopeless; finally, in a flurry of inspiration, he thought of the left-luggage office at Paddington Station. He bought a cheap suitcase (totally unworthy of its precious contents but it couldn't be helped) and deposited the lot. He had not the faintest idea what he could do with them later, he didn't even think about it. He had an appointment with Destiny at the party, he felt; and Destiny could surely take care of a few articles of clothing.

'I'll be late tonight darling,' he said to Anne at breakfast on the morning of the party, 'Sales Department booze-up. Don't worry about me, just go to bed.'

'But Jamie,' said Anne plantively, 'you know I've got to rehearse the carol concert, and Sue can only stay till eight and I told her you'd relieve her then, I know I went through it all with you – Cressida don't put egg in your pocket – can't you possibly get out of it or at least come home early?'

'Sorry, no,' said James, amazed at his own firmness, and fixing his mind firmly on the suitcase at Paddington and its contents to lend him further courage. 'No I can't. Dominic stop that at once, I don't want your Ribena. You'll just have to get someone else to babysit for you, Anne, I'm afraid; I'm sorry.'

'But it's not for me, it's for us,' said Anne looking at him in astonishment at this piece of heresy. 'They're your children, not just mine.'

'True,' said James, picking up his briefcase and the paper, 'but it's your carol concert. Bye darling.'

Anne watched him going down the path and then started clearing up very slowly. He hadn't been the same since she had found the socks.

The clothes were a bit creased when he got them out of the suitcase but there was nothing he could do about that. He hung them up rather boldy behind his office door and hoped they would look better by six o'clock. They did.

He had his hair cut rather expensively at lunch time, feeling there was no point leaving the icing off the cake – or rather too much on it – at this stage; he promised Anne mentally as he paid the outrageous bill that he would go without lunch for two months to make up for it.

He waited until most people had gone home, changed in the men's cloakroom, put his own clothes in the suitcase and took it back to the station. Then he took a taxi down to Sloane Street.

He was no longer nervous; he felt, in his new clothes, so different, so absolutely another person, that what he was doing and where he was going seemed entirely right and appropriate, but he did feel an enormous sense of excitement and anticipation, as if he was off to meet some beloved person from whom he had been too long separated.

When he arrived the party was half complete. James stood in the doorway, holding the glass of champagne he had been handed, simply gazing into the room. Here surely was Elysium, a glittering, glossy paradise: beautiful women, rich men (some of them beautiful too), fine clothes, brittle conversation. He caught snatches of it, as people passed him by: 'Darling . . . such heaven . . . you look marvellous, what have you been doing . . . did you see his last exhibition . . . frightfully overrated . . . Aspen for Christmas . . . new husband . . . absurd divorce case . . . with a wife like that who needs a mistress . . . absolutely broke . . . sold all his mother's shares . . . tiny house in Nice, do come . . .'

It was like the music of the spheres, and he would have stood there all evening, perfectly content, quite careless of the fact that he could not contribute even a note, had not someone suddenly pushed past him, trodden on his foot, and overbalanced, tipping the entire contents of a glass of champagne down his shirt. And then a voice: 'Oh God how absolutely ghastly, I am so sorry, how could I have done such a stupid thing, oh look at your shirt, and it's so beautiful too, what can I do to make amends? Come with me, come on, Jonathan Jonathan, where are you, look it's too awful, look what I've done to this poor man's shirt.'

James felt a hand on his arm, and then saw it sliding

down to take his own: a small white hand, it was, with long red nails, and wearing a selection of fine gold twisty rings. Following the line of the hand up the arm, his eyes took in fine black crepe (cut away to show much fine white bosom), a mane of streaked blonde hair, and a face which could only be described as beautiful, smiling at him encouragingly as its owner pulled him through the crowd.

'Now,' thought James, 'now if only I could die now, this instant, and I need never see this ending,' and afterwards, as he relived the evening a thousand, ten thousand times, he pinpointed that moment as the one he became actually part of the Glimpses, albeit only as associate member.

But he did not die; he found himself alive and rather wet in a small kitchen behind the gallery with the owner of the hand and the arm and the bosom and the face dabbing rather helplessly at his shirt and still shouting for Jonathan.

'Where is the silly sod?' she said crossly. 'Talking to some rich Arab, I expect. He's never around when I need him.'

'Er, who is Jonathan?' asked James, thinking he had better at least test his voice and show that he was not actually mute.

'Jonathan, oh, he's my boyfriend,' she said, 'and he owns the gallery, don't you know him then, I thought everyone here did.'

'Well no, not really,' said James and then, terrified lest his credentials weren't going to meet her scrutiny, 'I'm here because I bought a picture once.'

'Oh really, whose?' she asked, recommencing her dabbing. 'Oh, dear, this isn't doing any good, not this creep who's on now, I hope, terrible waste of money, Jonathan, oh there you are, what on earth have you beeing doing, look I've spilt champagne all over this poor man's lovely shirt, what can we do, is it covered by insurance, do you think?'

'I shouldn't think so,' said Jonathan, looking slightly coldly at James and his shirt. 'Awfully sorry about it of course, but it'll dry clean OK. You shouldn't have stood anywhere near Georgina, she's hopelessly accident-prone, she's always spilling something over somebody, last time it was best claret over me. At least champagne doesn't show.'

'Oh Jonathan, you are a bastard,' said Georgina, hurling the cloth at him. 'How can you be so unkind, you deserve to be sued. Now look,' she said to James, 'let me at least get you some more champagne. Acutally Jonathan is right, champagne doesn't usually stain, but do get it cleaned and send him the bill. He's quite right, I am hopelessly accident-prone, you wouldn't believe the things I do, I drove my own car over my own bicycle the other night, which didn't do either of them much good. Now look, here's some more champagne. What do you do? I mean, are you a writer or a collector or something terribly glamorous?'

'Er, not exactly,' said James, wondering wildly what he could claim, and settling for the near-truth. 'I'm in . . . well, finance.'

'Oh,' she said instantly losing interest, 'a banker. I thought you looked a bit different.'

'Well I'm not quite a banker,' said James eagerly and truthfully, 'it's more – well, insurance in a way.'

In every way, he thought, and thought also that he could

hardly have said anything more boring. But it seemed not: she brightened up at once. 'Oh,' she said, 'oh, how wonderful. That's amazing, you might be able to help me. Listen could you possibly, do you think, spare me an hour one day next week to come to my flat, I've just bought a pair of Victorian seascapes, and I'm desperate to get them valued and insured, I think I've been rather clever and they're a bit special, and Jonathan only knows about this sort of tricksy rubbish, he won't even look at them, and the man who usually insures my stuff won't have the faintest idea, he's an absolute philistine. I mean do you know anything about Victorian paintings at all, it's a new field to me.'

'Well, I do actually,' said James, thinking there must be indeed a God and a good one moreover. 'Not a lot, but enough to – well, advise you.'

'Oh marvellous,' she said, clasping his hand (so that once again the contents lapped perilously near the edge of the glass). 'Wonderful. So would you, could you, come and have a look at them? Or I could bring them to you, to your office, only they're a bit delicate really, the frames are disintegrating. And I'd probably drop them on the way.'

'Oh no, I'll come to your flat,' said James, trying to sound as if he received such invitations every day, 'really I don't mind a bit.'

'You are simply too kind,' said Georgina, 'really I couldn't be more grateful. Now look, I'd better go and circulate a bit or Jonathan will sulk all tomorrow, he's so bad-tempered. Have you got a card or anything so I know where to ring? No, look, it's you who's doing the favour, so you ring me, here's my number, whenever it suits you. I'm usually there till twelve, and then I go to my class, and then various other places, so it's best to ring early. But really any time will do, I'm sure you're in thousands of desperately high-powered meetings all the time, I do think it's so kind of you.'

'No, honestly,' said James, 'it's nothing, really, I'd like to do it.'

'You're sweet,' she said, standing on tiptoe and kissing his cheek. 'I'll wait to hear from you. And I really am so sorry about your shirt. All right, Jonathan, I'm coming . . .'

James left almost at once. He wanted to preserve the perfection of the evening, to place it in some untouchable place in his mind, before it became smudged or even blurred. He walked for hours; up Sloane Street, through the park, down Mount Street and into Bond Street, and he sat for some time on one of the seats near Asprey's, gazing at his expensive shoes and remembering with painstaking care every moment of the evening behind him. The Glimpses had been all, more, than he had ever dreamt; and he felt not as if he had been in some strange alien place but rather that he had come safely and at long last home.

And so his strange new life began. He replaced his clothes in the suitcase in the Gents at Paddington, replaced the case in the left-luggage office yet again, and then caught the 10.13 home. It seemed astonishing that he could have journeyed so far and so fast, and yet not even be on the last train. Anne was back from choir practice and whirring somewhat aggressively at the sewing machine.

'It's the angels' robes for the playgroup nativity concert,' she said slightly coldly when he asked her what she was making. 'I told you I had to make them all. Tomorrow I have to start on the haloes. Nobody else was prepared to take them on, and there's only ten days to go. How was the party?'

'Oh fine,' said James, going quickly into the kitchen. 'You know what these things are like.'

'No, actually I don't,' said Anne, and no actually, you don't, thought James and, as with the price of the Paul Smith tie, the thought gave him immense pleasure.

He telephoned Georgina on Tuesday rather than Monday, not wishing to appear gauche or even in possession of too much time.

'Hallo,' she said, when she answered the phone. 'Yes, who is this?'

'Oh,' said James, 'it's the man from the party.'

'Which party?' she said, sounding puzzled, and he realized that far from the party being the highest pinnacle of her social career, as it had been for him, it was probably one of many identical small mounds.

'Oh, you know,' he said, 'the one at the gallery. You spilt champagne down my shirt.'

'Oh, God yes, how kind of you to ring, you're going to insure my paintings. Wonderful. How's the shirt?'

'Oh, it's fine,' said James, thinking of it rather sadly as it lay, uncared for and slightly smelly, in the suitcase. 'Really, no damage.'

'Oh, good,' said Georgina, 'Jonathan was right; he usually is, it's such a drag. Now when can you come round?'

'Well, how's tomorrow?' asked James.

'Perfect,' she said. 'Come about eleven, and then I'll buy you lunch afterwards, to say thank you.'

'Oh no, you mustn't,' said James, horrified at the thought of more appalling sartorial shortfall. He could just about, he thought, get away with his very best suit for looking at the paintings, but there was no conceivable way he could wear it out to lunch in the Land of the Glimpses.

'Yes, I absolutely insist,' said Georgina. 'It's the least I can do. Now my address is 17 Boltons Grove. It's just off the Boltons, garden flat. See you tomorrow.'

An hour later saw James in a state of wretched ecstasy in Austin Reed, his Barclaycard growing very warm in his pocket, buying a suit. He did seem to have good taste, he thought, and more surprisingly, to be able to wear clothes well; in a dark-grey pinstripe, and a white-and-grey striped shirt, he could hold his satorial own against Jonathan any day. These at least he would be able to take home, Anne would never know what they'd cost, and then he could smuggle the shoes in a month or so later. He was beginning to enjoy the whole thing.

'Oh, hallo,' said Georgina, dressed in a bath towel and looking slightly surprised as she opened the door to him next day (he had pleaded toothache in the office). 'Gosh, is that the time already? I've only just got up. Come in, would you like a coffee or something?'

'Yes please,' said James, looking round with interest. Georgina's flat was exactly as he had known it would be while being totally unpredictable (how uncomfortably well he understood this new world. It was as if he had been a changeling, stolen away at birth by suburban fairies. He liked that thought, it charmed him and made him feel less guilty). White everywhere, with high ceilings, and marble floors; in the drawing room an exquisite Indian carpet hung on one of the walls, two tall carved screens stood in either corner of the room, and a heavy wrought-iron chandelier with tall white candles in it hung from the ceiling; a slightly surprising raspberry pink sofa set in the window bay lent the room wit. There were two Chiparus bronzes, a Lalique brass lamp and an art nouveau rocking chair; two enormous ferns spilt out of a pair of pure white jardinières. James stood drinking it in, like a starving man; he could hardly tear his eyes from it even to go into the kitchen (all black and white, not a splinter of pine to be seen), where Georgina was calling to him to fetch his coffee.

'Could you bear to wait just three minutes while I get dressed?' she said. 'And then I'll show you the pictures.'

'Yes that's fine,' said James. 'No hurry, really you go ahead.' He would have waited three hours and happily, but in almost exactly three minutes she was back, wearing jeans and a grey silk shirt. She really was most beautiful: quite tall and very slim, her eyes so dark blue they were almost navy, 17 her hair a wild blonde mane. She could have been any age from eighteen to twenty-five; boldly he told her so, and she laughed.

'I'm just twenty-one, the flat was a birthday present, do you like it?'

'Very much, yes,' said James, anxious to appear as one to whom a flat in the Boltons was an absolutely standard birthday present. 'But where are the paintings?'

'Oh, they're here,' she said, and dragged them out from under one of the sofas. 'Now what do you think? More coffee?'

'No thank you,' said James, looking at the pictures. They were fairly ordinary seascapes: pretty and a little unusual, but not worth more than £300 the pair.

'Oh dear, I can tell, they're worthless aren't they?' said Georgina.

'Well not worthless, but not worth much,' said James truthfully, 'not worth insuring separately anyway, you should just get them included on your existing policy.'

'Oh, damn, and I was so sure I'd made a real find,' said Georgina. 'Now that bastard Jonathan will laugh at me. Oh well, back to the drawing board. Gosh, it's nearly time for my class.'

James had been wondering what the class could be; Anne was always attending classes, and as well as her course in Communications, she had done Upholstery, Child Development and Literary Appreciation, none of which seemed likely Glimpse studies; he noticed that Georgina had a leotard lying over one of the chairs.

'Are you a dancer?' he asked.

'Oh heavens no. I'm an art dealer very manqué. As you can see. No, I go to dance class every day to keep my weight down. Now I haven't forgotten about lunch, I still want to take you, could you meet me at San Fred's at one fifteen? Please. Don't argue. Just come.'

San Frediano's was Glimpse country all right. Pretty, careless people sat at tables with other pretty, careless people, frequently darting across the room to greet, to kiss, to exclaim still more. James arrived deliberately early and sat at the table Georgina had thoughtfully booked, watching and absorbing. He was a quick study; in the twenty minutes he spent there he learnt a great deal about the group behaviour and sexual signalling of the breed he was studying. When Georgina arrived, he took her hand and kissed her cheek. 'I missed you,' he said.

'Do you know,' she said, sparkling up at him, 'I don't even know your name.'

'My name,' said James, sipping a glass of champagne he had taken it upon himself to order, 'is James. What else would you like to know?'

Two hours later they were both rather drunk. Georgina had knocked over two glasses of wine and spilt her sauce down her silk shirt; she sat, her thigh pressed hard against James's, her hand moving rather agitatedly in his, and her dark blue eyes fixed on his grey ones with some degree of intensity.

'Tell me,' she said. 'Could your company manage 19

without you for another hour or so? Because I don't think I can.'

'Oh yes,' said James, 'I'm quite sure it could. Let's get a taxi.'

In the taxi he felt suddenly nervous. The strictly paced, absolutely predictable routine he went through with Anne every six days was the only sexual experience he had known for many years; he did not feel it really equipped him to move the earth or even a tiny bit of the Boltons with this beautiful hungry person.

Undressing (and oh, dear, he thought, more anxiously wretched than ever, the shirt and suit might be Austin Reed, but the vest and Y-fronts were Marks and Spencer and a baggy three years old at that) he felt worse and worse, and became totally silent, feeling foolish.

But Georgina did not seem to be caring very much, either about the Y-fronts or the silence. She lay on her bed (even in his hour of trial he noticed that the head of it was cast iron, art nouveau and undoubtedly worth a fortune), her own slightly too skinny body absolutely naked; and she held out her arms as he lay down and kissed her forehead in a gesture of extraordinary sweetness. What followed was quite outside his experience in levels of passion and delight, but he did not feel clumsy or nervous, it was as if some powerfully invading sexual force had entered him that he might enter her. It was a triumph and a glory and afterwards he thought that for the first time he had truly understood what it meant to make love.

'Goodness me,' said Georgina, as they lay smiling at one another. 'I hope your company has a good policy out on you.'

'I'm afraid,' said James with perfect truth, 'that they wouldn't mind if I died tomorrow.'

'Oh, nonsense,' said Georgina, 'I'm sure they must be hugely dependent on you. Now listen, I have to go in about ten minutes, to the gallery to see some idiot painter with Jonathan. And you, I suppose, have to go back to your important job and then home to your lovely kind maternal wife.'

'I'm afraid I do,' said James, thinking with some dread of the metamorphosis that had to be gone through before he got home; rather like a speeded-up film he watched himself phoning from a call box 'tooth out, really painful, going straight home', the tube journey to Paddington, the exchange of his new shoes for his old at the left luggage office (his suit was quite enough to explain for one week), the dreary trundle home on the 6.13 having killed a couple of hours in the buffet bar and then 'hallo-darling-had a good-day-need-any help-up-there' as he got into the bath time, story time and babysitting while Anne went to fulfil her duties as treasurer of the Residents Association.

It was all right at first; he thought himself dutifully into his proper role – or rather improper, as he increasingly felt it to be – towelled down small plump bodies (to the accompaniment of some disturbing images of a larger skinny one) read *Winnie the Pooh* and dutifully ate sausages and mash despite his tastebuds being still tuned to quails' eggs and champagne. Later he helped Anne make lanterns for the shepherds in the Nativity Play, commiserated with her over being landed with making all the quiches for the PTA supper and barn dance, and fell asleep in front of the television while she was out. But later, when she had come back and was making their bedtime cocoa, he remembered with a thud of anxiety that this was the Sixth, if not the Seventh night and the Laura Ashley nightie would undoubtedly be unbuttoned. It was; he closed his eyes and thought of the Boltons and got through it somehow. Not splendidly but just about competently; afterwards he mumbled something about being tired and fell into a confused sleep. Life might be beautiful amongst the Glimpses, but it was dreadfully demanding.

And expensive too, he thought, looking aghast at his Barclaycard statement two months later. From a fairly respectable £162 at the beginning of December, it had now soared into a very nasty looking £1260 with a note at the bottom that said, 'Please send at least £90 to clear the excess over your credit limit. Do not use your card further without authority,' and a list of purchases that would have made a wonderful case for a prosecuting divorce lawyer. Clothes, meals, flowers and wine all sat upon it in extravagant splendour; the suitcase in the left-luggage office was bursting at its tacky seams.

He was worried all the time; he worried about money, worried about his job (which he was neglecting terribly), worried about his marriage; he was perpetually tired, chronically confused (who am I today, this morning, tomorrow night), and permanently and rapturously happy.

For the impossible had happened and he and Georgina had fallen in love. He had not known love before, he realized; had not experienced the delicate uncurling of tenderness, the steady powerful growth of joy, the insistent pounding of desire, the explosion of need to be with the beloved every available moment of every existing hour. What he had felt for Anne had been a decorous, carefully chosen piece of furniture for his life; what he knew for Georgina was a total demolition of everything that could be deemed right and proper and a restructure into new, beautiful, unrecognizable territory.

At first he had not been able to believe that she loved him in return, he had thought she must be simply amusing herself, but she did, she told him so day after dizzy day, and grew paler and even thinner, while assuring him of her happiness and her contentment with the way things were. She had given up Jonathan, she had stopped wanting to go to parties; she simply waited, infinitely patient, for the times they could be together.

James found the transition from one life to another more and more difficult to make, the contrast increasingly painful and sharp. Although he had stopped pretending totally to Georgina, had told her some of the truth (that he did not actually quite belong with the Glimpses, that he was not in fact very important or rich) he still felt and indeed became, metamorphosed when he was with her into somebody quite different and in whom he was beginning 23 rather dangerously to believe.

Every meeting, every lunch, every rare outing put him further in love, but it did something else too, more ridiculous, less innocent: it made him more deeply committed to, more totally besotted with, Georgina's lifestyle. And he had no right to that; he had earned her, perhaps, by way of words and loving and lovemaking, but not the rest. He was helplessly, hopelessly in debt, and worse than in debt, in thrall. The Glimpses had become sorcerers, they had cast a spell on him, and he could not escape.

The cruch came of course, it had to, sneaking up on him like some sinister, predatory beast.

It was not a love letter that gave him away, as they do in books, nor a well-meaning friend as they do in real life; not even his Barclaycard statement, his diary, or even the labels on his new shirts. It was a ticket from the left-luggage office at Paddington Station.

The children found it; they were playing with his wallet one Saturday morning, as he tried rather wearily to concentrate on what Anne was telling him about the new Neighbourhood Watch scheme, and he realized too late that they had actually extracted the ticket, along with a five-pound note and his driving licence and were playing a game of cards with them all on the table.

'Children give those to me, at once,' he said, just a little too sharply; Anne looked up, aware of the urgency in his tone, saw the expression on his face, and then looked down at the table.

'What on earth have you got in the left-luggage office?' she said.

'Oh, nothing. Nothing much,' said James. He was sweating; he reached out for the coffee pot and tried to control his shaking hand.

'What do you mean nothing? Why should you have anything there? Why can't you tell me?'

'Of course I can tell you. It's just – well, my briefcase. With some rather important work in. There's nowhere I can keep anything safe in this bloody shambles. I put it there for the weekend.'

'James, don't be ridiculous. You've got the office. You're lying. What on earth is in the left-luggage office at Paddington Station that you can't tell me about?'

'Oh, darling,' said James, in a last desperate attempt to escape from the vice that was holding him. 'Just some work. And – and some wine,' he added, beginning to stammer, 'some wine for next Thursday, when your parents are coming round. I couldn't carry it, so I left it until I had the car. All right?'

'No,' said Anne. 'Not all right. You're lying. And if you won't tell me what's there, I want to go and see for myself.' She was flushed and breathing very heavily; her eyes were brilliant and fixed on his face.

'I'm going to Paddington,' she said, 'now. Do you want to come with me or not?' James nodded helplessly. 'Come along, children, we're all going out.'

They drove to Paddington in silence. The children were quiet, sensing a drama. James felt terribly sick. There was 25 nothing now that he could do. Anne was going to open Pandora's box in the middle of Paddington station, and the demons inside were deadly indeed.

They didn't look deadly, just rather odd. Three silk shirts, two of them slightly smelly; a suit; two pairs of shoes; a jacket; a Gucci wallet and cashmere sweater. Anne looked at them, looked at him, and then picked out the wallet. Inside was a bill for lunch at the Savoy, and a note in Georgina's handwriting. 'Thank you for the best two hours of my whole life,' it said.

'You creep,' was all she said, and then walked away to the car and the children, leaving James to journey home alone on the train.

He did think of ringing Georgina, but it seemed a messy point to do it at. He preferred to wait until at least something had been resolved.

When he finally got home, Anne was making bread as she always did when she was worried or upset; indeed the smell of baking, far from typifying calm and comfort to James always meant trouble, ranging in severity from a difficult committee meeting to a bad attack of PMT. He stood silent, waiting for her to speak.

'I don't want to talk about it now,' she said, very cold and calm. 'We'll wait until the children are in bed.'

'The children?' he said, 'don't you think this is more important than the children?'

She looked at him with such dislike, such contempt, that his knees literally gave way beneath him and he had to sit
26 down. 'I personally don't think anything is more important

than the children,' she said, 'and certainly not your squalid, well-dressed adultery.'

She had always had a way with words.

'I have decided,' said Anne, finally sitting down that evening with a glass of wine and a very determined expression, 'that the best thing is for you to stay, at least for a while, so we can work things out. There's no point acting hastily. Obviously I am partly to blame, this sort of thing is never just one person's fault. I am quite happy to talk it through and find out what's gone wrong, and see what we can do to put things right again.'

'I should be feeling grateful,' thought James, wondering why he wasn't. 'I should be kissing her feet, saying I'm sorry, begging for forgiveness. But I'm not.'

'I don't want to hear about her,' Anne went on. 'I can't see the point. In fact I'd rather not. As long as you promise me never to see her again, then that can be the end of her as far as I'm concerned. I've no wish to know what she looks like or does, or what she has to offer. I can't see what good it would do. Obviously it's been a difficult time for you, but we must just try to put it behind us. You can't undo the past, after all.'

James looked at her sitting there, smiling carefully, not crying, not applying emotional blackmail, in her cosy battered chair where she had breastfed and cuddled and comforted the children, and mended their clothes and made out lists for Sainsbury's and written minutes of meetings, good Anne, kind Anne, well organized, loyal, blind Anne, and he knew that he had to tell her, that there was no point trying to be kind, attempting to spare her, selling her a soft option. He had to dish up the truth, raw, unseasoned, unpalatable, and force her to swallow it.

'I'm sorry,' he said, 'but you have to hear about her. About all of it. I just have to tell you. You have to understand.'

Anne stopped looking determined and started looking nervous. She had found a pink once-fluffy rabbit stuffed down her chair, and she started picking at its bare patches, making them bigger, less neat. James looked at it, and thought it symbolized their marriage, getting balder and more hideous every moment.

'To start with,' he said, 'I can't possibly promise never to see her again. I love her. I'm sorry and I can't help it, but that's the fact of the matter. And more important probably is for you to hear what she has to offer. That will do some good, because it will make you see why we can't put things right. What Georgina, that's her name, what she has to offer, is a way of life. The way of life I need, that suits me. The life we have been sharing, you and I, is not right for me. I know that now. And I can't stay in it. It's stifling me. I need something more – well, more adult.'

'I see,' said Anne. She was looking at him with an odd expression that was half distaste, half something quite different. Had James been a little less overwrought he might have recognized it as humour.

'That is precisely what Georgina has to offer me, you see,' he said. 'An adult life. A life with some beauty in it. A selfish life if you like. And it is the only life I can bear to lead now. I am desperately sorry, I can see I must seem hideously ungrateful, and you shall have every penny I can possibly give you, I shall visit the children if you will let me whenever I can, but I can't go on living here.'

Anne gazed at him blankly for a while and then said 'I see' for a second time. That was the end of their marriage.

It was not that neat and tidy of course. The hostilities actually went on for some time; Anne's calm exploded into a noisy, anguished outrage, and James's cool reason deserted him from time to time; but at the end of it they met; they gazed at each other over the dreadful irony of the head of the youngest child, awakened by the noise and now asleep again on his mother's lap, and managed to smile, exhaustedly, weakly, but at least not entirely estranged.

Anne then took the child to bed with her, closing the door gently behind her; and so, his marriage seeming to him thus most poignantly epitomized, James walked very quietly out of the door, into the car and drove to Georgina's flat.

He stopped on the way to phone her, to tell her no more than that he was coming; she had some friends with her but promised to get rid of them before he got there, and he feasted his mind desperately on her, and how he would find her, how he needed to find her.

The journey he was making symbolized the whole of his past life; away from the laurel hedges, the gravel drives, the estate cars, the quiet safe streets, and into the dazzling, hustling busy-ness of Saturday night London. He had left the womb he had inhabited for so long, so warm, so cosy, so increasingly uncomfortable, and been thrust into a new, bright, hard-edged world where he might be fighting for his life, but where at least the life was what he wanted. He knew it wasn't going to remain so simple, so clear-cut; there would be endless journeys back to the womb, half-felt regrets. There would be dreadful financial difficulties, legal unpleasantness and sorrowing faces, and the loss of much love. But for this hour, this night, he allowed himself the luxury of seeing it simply, of having chosen what he wanted, done battle for it and won.

Tonight he would be where he belonged, cleaved finally to the Glimpses; in a white flat in Kensington with not a bottle of Ribena in a half-mile radius, where the Fisher Prices must be the nice new couple at number 92 and the only cries in the night were adult and orgasmic.

Exhausted and exalted, he reached the Boltons, parked the car, ran down the steps, rang the bell. Georgina fell into his arms; beyond her stood paradise, quiet, peaceful, beautiful . . .

'What is it?' she said, 'what has happened, tell me, tell me everything.'

'I've done it,' he said weakly, collapsing on to the pink sofa. 'I've left her. I'm here to stay. If you'll have me.'

'Oh, my darling,' said Georgina, 'as if I wouldn't.' She paused and looked at him, her navy-blue eyes huge and starry. 'I have some wonderful news too. I'm going to have a baby . . .'

Glass Slipper

Cinderella Case jury out. Verdict expected this afternoon

Eleanor Charteris looked at the newspaper placards and then at the man sitting beside her in the taxi. He managed a rather weak smile.

'I feel sick,' he said. 'How about you?'

'A bit,' she said. 'I know it's still very much in the balance. But either way we've done well. The general public certainly thinks you should be the winner. So . . .'

'The general public aren't going to pay me damages. Or costs.'

'No but you've had some brilliant publicity,' said Eleanor briskly. 'You'll get more work than you can ever handle in the future. And everyone's singing the wretched song. It's at Number One again this week. So if we do win . . .'

'Yes, I know. Money coming out of our ears. You've been marvellous, Eleanor. Absolutely marvellous. I still don't know quite why you decided to take the case on. When it looked so absolutely hopeless.'

'I might tell you one day,' said Eleanor. 'God, I hope this 31 traffic clears. It's almost two thirty. We can't be late for the judge.'

They stopped outside the law courts at 2.25 p.m. Eleanor paid off the cab. The driver waved at her and grinned, gave her the thumbs-up sign. 'You're the solicitor in this Cinderella case, aren't you?' he said. 'Hope you win. Show the bastard where he gets off. You can tell he's a cheat, just by looking at him.'

'Well, we shall have to see,' said Eleanor, smiling at him sweetly. 'But thank you for your good wishes anyway.'

She walked rather slowly into the law courts, and stood waiting for her client, who was making what she hoped was a suitably non-committal statement to the hordes of press at his heels. Some of the things he'd said recently had been a little over the top. He looked very drawn, very tired. Poor man. And then, coming down the corridor towards her in the opposite direction, looking neither drawn nor tired but outrageously confident and cheerful, she saw him. Smiling at her, his dark eyes moving over her face, lingering on her mouth; and the years rolled away and she was nineteen years old again, dressed in layers of white and pink lace, her hair an expensive tangle of dark curls, the udoubted belle of the ball and ready to fall helplessly in love with anyone who came her way; and to live out her own version of the Cinderella story.

'But I don't want to go the ball,' wailed Nell. 'I hate balls, you know I do, I hate all that stuff.'

'Darling, just to please your old godmother. I just want to have a few more young people there, it would help me so much. Charles Drummond-Browne will be there,' she added.

'But –' Nell hesitated, looked at her godmother; she was terribly fond of her, she hated upsetting her. But she knew exactly what this ball would be like, full of old people like her godmother, who must be at least fifty now, how could people of that age even think of dancing? There was something faintly obscene about it. And she did like Charles very much, he was so good-looking and clever – and extremely rich. Not that she cared about that of course, but . . .

'Go on, Eleanor,' said Ursula with an encouraging smile, sensing her weakening. 'I'll buy you a new dress. And pay for you to have your hair done.'

That really was irresistible. Nell's die-straight brown hair was the bane of her life. 'Oh – all right.'

'Darling, thank you. I'll meet you at Harvey Nicks this afternoon. Two o'clock, side entrance.'

She was late at the ball because her hair went wrong, and then she couldn't get a taxi; she rushed over to Ursula's table, breathless and apologetic, when everyone was about to start dinner. Charles, clearly torn between disapproval of her lateness and pleasure that she had finally arrived, stood up, smiling with his careful charm.

'Better late than never,' he said. 'Come and have some champagne.'

It was a very good evening; she danced and talked with Charles most of the time. She had known him for a couple of months, had spent a few slightly formal but very pleasant evenings with him, and was more than half convinced she was in love with him. He treated her with a rather old-fashioned courtesy, had kissed her fairly expertly and seemed to expect no more than that, which made a pleasant change. Most of the young men she knew assumed she was dying to get into bed with them in return for a pizza and a glass of cheap red wine. He was fifteen years older than she was, heir to a very old English baronetcy; he was a highly successful barrister. Nell's mother, who was a rather hard-up widow, was extremely excited at the prospect of the romance.

'You look lovely,' said Charles, smiling down at her, as they waltzed slightly formally round the floor. 'But then you always do.'

'Thank you,' said Nell.

'I'd – well, I'd like to see a lot more of you Nell. Would you like that?'

'Yes,' she said, smiling up at him, her heart leaping pleasantly. 'Yes Charles, I would.'

He pulled her closer. 'I'm a bit – well, old-fashioned, I know. I like to take things slowly. But – I do think about you a great deal. And look forward to seeing you. How about
34 you?'

Nell looked up at him, touched by his awkwardness, wanting to ease it.

'I feel just the same,' she said. She did. It wasn't rapture exactly, but it was very nice.

'Good,' he said, 'then we must proceed, take things further.'

She wondered, even in the midst of her pleasure, if that was how he talked to his clients in Chambers.

They were sitting at the table, smiling slightly foolishly at one another, when the cabaret was announced.

'Christ,' groaned Charles, 'a chanteuse, I suppose.'

But it wasn't a chanteuse, it was an extraordinarily handsome young man, in white tie and tails, his dark hair slicked back, who played the piano and sang 'thirties numbers with great charm; after an initial repertoire, he said he would take requests.

There were a lot of predictable ones, like 'Tea for Two' and 'Top Hat', and then Nell stood up and asked for 'Dancing on the Ceiling'. He looked at her blankly for a moment, then smiled and began to play. He was really very accomplished; after about three more numbers he played 'Dance Little Lady' as an encore, and then came over to Nell's table, smiling.

'Well done,' he said. 'You almost had me there. Can I claim a dance as prize?'

'Oh – yes,' said Nell, looking anxiously at Charles, who nodded just slightly coolly first at her, then the young man. 'Yes, thank you.'

He danced very well; Nell promptly felt she had not two but three left feet.

'Relax,' he said, and then, as the music changed, 'here's a slow one. Let's talk. What's your name?'

'It's Eleanor,' said Nell, 'but everyone calls me Nell.'

'I shall call you Ella. As in Cinder-Ella. So appropriate for the belle of the ball. Which you certainly are. I hope you won't vanish at midnight.'

'I promise I won't,' said Nell. 'And you are?'

'Nick. Nick Buitoni. You could call me Buttons, I suppose. As I'm here strictly in a Below Stairs capacity – I'm sure I'm not meant to dance with the guests.'

'Well I'm glad you did,' said Nell, and meant it.

'That's a peach of a dress.'

'Thank you.'

'And those earrings are wonderful. Pure deco. Where did you get them?'

'Jumble sale,' said Nell. 'Pure paste, I'm sure.'

'They suit you. Is that your boyfriend, watching us like a rather disapproving hawk?'

'Oh – yes. Yes it is,' said Nell. For some reason she felt less happy at the idea than she had ten minutes earlier.

Suddenly he stopped dancing, took her face in his hands, and kissed her gently on the mouth.

'You're lovely,' he said.

The most extraordinary sensation ripped through Nell: a piercing sweetness, half pleasure, half almost pain. She closed her eyes, kissed him back, just briefly, then pulled away, staring at him, shocked, shaken. Out of the corner of her eye she saw Charles, frozen-faced, calling her over, slightly imperiously.

'I'd better go,' she said to Nick Buitoni, her voice sounding strange even to herself. 'I am supposed to be with him.'

'Of course,' he said. 'Goodbye Cinderella. I hope we'll meet again.'

It wasn't until she was in the Ladies much later on that she realised she had dropped one of her earrings.

Eleanor became Mrs. Charles Drummond-Browne a year later in a lavish ceremony at St. Margaret's, Westminster; the reception for 700 people (paid for at her charming insistence by her new mother-in-law) took place at Claridges, and they went to the Drummond-Brownes' shooting lodge in Scotland for a fortnight before Charles had to return to Chambers. The honeymoon was chilly in more ways than one; Charles as a lover was dutiful and competent rather than inspired. More than once, to her horror, Nell found herself thinking of Nick Buitoni and the sweet probing warmth that had flooded through her when he kissed her at the ball, and wondered if she would ever know it again.

Nevertheless, when they returned to London she was pregnant with Flora, and two years later presented Charles with the Honourable James Drummond-Browne, the heir to his title and estates. By then she was fairly unhappy.

'We have to go the Red Cross Ball,' said Charles. 'I know it's a bore, but old Geoffrey Blagdon asked if we'd join his table and I couldn't say no. Three weeks from tomorrow I think he said. Is that all right?'

'Well yes, I suppose so,' said Nell. 'And anyway, what if it wasn't?'

'Oh for heaven's sake, darling, don't start that. I was just trying to sound considerate.'

'How kind.'

'And this time do you think you could make a huge effort to actually talk to Molly Blagdon, rather than just sitting there staring at your plate? It's highly embarrassing.'

'Charles, what am I supposed to say to her? She treats me like some kind of moronic child.'

'Maybe that's because you appear to her like a moronic child. I don't know, Nell. If you haven't worked out some dinner-table conversation by now, there seems very little hope of it ever happening.'

'Thanks,' said Nell, getting up from the table so that he wouldn't see the easy tears rising behind her eyes, and wondering where the breezy, self-confident person who had walked down the aisle to marry Charles had gone.

'Ah, Eleanor, you're sitting next to me. How nice. Come and tell me what you've been doing. You're looking a bit peaky, my dear, doesn't young Charles look after you properly?'

That just summed it up, thought Nell. He didn't look after her in any way at all; not emotionally, not physically, not intellectually. He treated her increasingly like some kind of rather irksome responsibility – even in bed. Most of all in bed. She couldn't actually remember when she had last enjoyed sex.

She smiled determinedly at Geoffrey Blagdon. 'Yes of course he does. But the weather's been so beastly lately, I've hardly been out. You look wonderful,' she added carefully.

'Well, thank you my dear. Don't often get a compliment from a pretty girl. Promise me the first dance, won't you?'

'Yes of course,' said Nell.

'I don't believe it,' said a voice. That voice. That lovely, sexy, warm voice. 'Cinderella. Back at the ball. You did vanish, that night. I came looking for you and I couldn't find you.'

Nell sat frozen to her chair, afraid even to turn round at first in case he was a hallucination, so often had she imagined this moment. Then she did turn, slowly, looked up, and there he was, a little older, but just as handsome, just as vividly, dangerously attractive.

'Hallo,' was all she managed to say.

'You're a lot thinner. Marriage doesn't seem to agree with you. I read about it in the papers, your grand wedding to your Prince Charming. Are you all right?'

'Yes of course,' she said, illogically indignant. 'And you?'

'Oh, I'm fine. Still struggling. Not played the Palladium yet. Now look, I have something of yours. Here. I never go anywhere without it, just in case I find you. Now I wonder if 39 it fits, and then I shall know . . .'

'Know what, if what fits?' said Nell, laughing, and then stared incredulously as Nick Buitoni produced from his pocket, wrapped carefully in a slightly yellowing silk handkerchief, a dangly paste earring.

'You dropped it when you fled. Here, put it on.'

'I can't,' said Nell laughing. 'I'm wearing my mother-in-law's diamonds. Charles wouldn't like it.'

'Charles isn't going to get it,' said Nick Buitoni lightly. 'Well take it anyway. And come and dance with me. I seem to remember Cinderella and Buttons had a high old time of it in the kitchen.'

'Better than she had with the prince probably,' said Nell with a sigh.

'You sound sad,' said Nick. 'Come along and tell me about it.'

Nell looked round; Charles was talking what was clearly business at another table. He wouldn't notice. And if he did he wouldn't care. She stood up, took his hand. A charge went through her, the same sweet warmth she remembered, still, after all these years. She followed him onto the floor and decided fate could take matters over.

Fate propelled her into love: wild, tender, shaking, laughing, crying love. Nick Buitoni persuaded her into bed after a series of very long, seductive lunches, bombarding her with the full force of his considerable sexuality. Trying to analyse it afterwards, the nearest Nell came to describing that sexuality was that it was as cerebral as it was physical, he talked her into desire, used words, images, ideas that left her as weak and helpless against him as his mouth on hers, his hands moving over her, his body leading her to places and pleasures she had never even dreamed of. He had a studio flat in Highgate: a classically untidy bachelor place, with virtually no furniture except a huge bed, a low table, some big cushions, an old distinctly honky-tonk piano and a superbly equipped kitchen, part of the main room, where he cooked small exquisite delicacies for eating after love, washed down with champagne brought by Nell. He played music, wonderful music, 'music to love to' he said, Mahler, Bach, Puccini, and sometimes the 'thirties music they both loved. Nell came alive in that room, learnt what happiness meant; she felt she was owed it, she felt no guilt, just a sense of rightness. Nick had no other girl friends, he said, had just finished with someone 'and then I went back to waiting for you.'

He earned the little money he had playing the piano and singing in nightclubs, and places like the Savoy, so he was always free for her in the day: 'You see, Ella, my darling, our lives are made for each other, we can live in the kitchen just like Buttons and his Cinders.'

The intrigue and deceit excited her, didn't really make her feel bad at all. It was easy to invent stories about her long absences at lunch time; she was heavily involved in charity work and one more committee meeting every week or so was hardly going to excite suspicion. They evolved a code; she would ring his number and if he was out, she would say

Mrs Green at the Ealing number had called, could he ring her; nothing could be further from Lady Drummond-Browne of Chester Square, sw1 and Marley Park, Somerset than Mrs Green from Ealing. And he would announce himself to her (or the nanny or the housekeeper) in a thin South London drawl as Brian Smethers, or in a rich West Country roll as Dick Lacey. They invented lifestyles for Brian, who was an accountant's clerk working on one of her charities, and for Dick, who was a designer working on brochures for the many events she helped organise. It all added to the fun. Sometimes she rang him in the evening when she knew he was working, just to hear his voice. It sounded so exactly like him, that voice, she could see him at once, vividly, his untidy handsome face, the dark brown eyes, (so different from Charles' icy blue), the wild black hair, the ridiculously perfect teeth, the tall, rangy body (so unlike Charles' ramrod straight one) and she would listen smiling to the silly message: 'You have reached the answering machine of Nick Buitoni. I am out on a doubtless abortive mission to obtain work on stage, screen or the airwaves. Please leave your name and number, and I'll get back to you. Callers from Hollywood should contact my agent. Thanks for ringing.'

One day, when she arrived he was sitting at the piano, picking out a tune; it was haunting, sweet and swinging at the same time. Ella went over to him, kissed him, and he pulled her onto his knee.

'Like this?' he said. 'I wrote it for you. It's called Cinderella. You can help me with the lyrics. What do you think about – listen – ' He began to sing '*Clock strikes, Midnight, Love is gone, Clock strikes, First light, Sad sweet song . . .*'

'It's terrible,' said Nell, laughing, 'but the music is lovely. Did you really write it?'

'Of course,' he said, his face hurt. 'What do you think I am, a rip-off artist?'

'You might be.'

'In that case, Cinders, I'm going to do some serious ripping off. Starting with that extremely expensive-looking sweater.'

1983

She could never imagine afterwards how she had endured it for so long, for almost two years, the old half-and-half life, the one fairy story, fantasy, the other real, the one so filled with love, the other so empty of it, the one so joyful, the other so bleak; how she had reconciled guilt and pleasure, hope and fear, how adept she had become at lying, pretending, at building elaborate deceits. She considered quite often giving him up, and rejected it, afraid before it had even begun of the pain, the emptiness, the sheer awfulness of life without him. And she also waited, half hopefully, half fearfully, for him to move things on, make them better; dreamed, longed for his voice telling her he wanted her to leave Charles, to marry him. Only it never came; and she was too much of a coward to work out why. 43

And meanwhile Charles became richer and more successful, and colder and more critical, and Flora and James
began to grow up. She tried and failed to persuade Charles
that she should take up some kind of career: weathered the
deaths of her mother and godmother in the same dreadful
year: watched her own face in the mirror grown thinner,
sharper, and wondered what was to become of her. And the
flat in Highgate seemed more home to her than the houses
in Chelsea and Somerset, and the time she spent there more
real, more important than the time she spent being Charles'
wife, and lies and deceit became such second nature to her
(she who had always been so truthful, so direct) that she
quite often found herself wondering who precisely she was
and where exactly she was supposed to be.

And then one day, Nell realised it was actually rather
more than four weeks since she had last had a period;
bought a kit and did a test; and found she was pregnant.

'Well never mind,' said Nick tenderly, holding her while
she wept, moaned, rocked with grief. 'It's not so bad. I hate
to think about it, but presumably you still sleep with the
Prince. It's probably his.'

'No,' said Nell, looking up at him, her face ravaged with
tears. 'No, you don't understand. He's had a vasectomy.'

1983

44   'Now can I just get this straight?' said Charles. He was

horribly, hideously calm. 'You've been having an affair. You're pregnant. And the father of your child doesn't want to marry you?'

Nell looked back; equally calm, surprised by her own courage.

'Yes. That's exactly right.'

'I may be a little old-fashioned, but what reason does he give?'

'I don't think I want to talk about that,' said Nell, crushing with sheer force of will the memory of Nick looking carefully, dramatically distraught, saying that of course he loved her, he always would, but he couldn't actually marry her, couldn't even take her permanently into his home, because – well, oh it was so hard for him to explain, but –'

'But what, Nick?' she had said, finding what people meant exactly when they said fear clutched at their hearts; her own felt stilled, halted in its beating, icy fingers closed round it, squeezing it so it could beat no more.

'Well darling, what kind of a husband would I make? What kind of a father? Feckless, useless, virtually umemployed, broke –'

'You don't seem exactly broke,' said Nell carefully, afraid of antagonising him even while rage and pain broke over her in equal proportions. 'You seem to be doing rather nicely actually, you've got that extremely expensive car, lots of new clothes, you've just been on that holiday to Mexico –'

'Ella, darling, please!' His dark eyes were hurt, shocked even. 'That's the first holiday I've had for five years. Surely you don't begrudge me that. And I do need the odd shirt, you know, I can't go round dressed in rags and I don't have rich husbands or even fairy godmothers to buy me things. But darling, it's you I'm thinking of, not me, what kind of life can I offer you and a baby, living here in this garret –'

'It's not a garret,' cried Ella in anguish. 'It's lovely. I'd adore it, and besides I'd get something from Charles obviously, and –'

She looked at him and saw an expression deep in his eyes, beyond the careful hurt and concern; it was wariness, watchfulness. He was fighting to survive, looking for an escape, and in that moment she knew there was no hope, no hope for her at all, and that while he had been the love of her life, she was nothing of the sort to him, just a foolish, spoilt wife, bored into adultery and probably boring him as well by now.

She took a deep breath and met his eyes, those clever actor's eyes, and said, 'Well, Nick, there's clearly no future continuing this discussion. You're right, I would hate it. Now that I know how you really feel. I won't trouble you any further. Goodbye Nick. Don't bother to show me out.'

'Ella!' he said, carefully concerned now. 'Darling Ella, you can't just go. I love you, I need you. Listen, darling, you don't have to have this baby, you know. We are living in the twentieth century. Have you thought about – sweetheart don't look at me like that, it upsets me . . .'

'Well I'm truly sorry about that,' said Nell, white-hot

rage whipping through her, wondering if she might actually hit him. 'I really would hate to think anything I did might upset you, Nick. I did think about it, having an abortion, of course I did, and I'll tell you what I thought, it was that there's only one person truly innocent in all this hideous mess and that's the baby. I'm afraid I couldn't do that, Nick, not even to save you from feeling upset.'

'Ella, darlng, don't be so angry. I didn't mean – oh God, why can't we just . . .'

'We, as you put it, can't do anything,' said Nell. 'There was never any question of any "we" in your life. There's only one person in your life, Nick Buitoni, and always will be, and you've very welcome to him.'

The pleasure she got out of delivering that sentence and the expression of profound shock on his face helped to see her out of the flat, into her car, and she had actually reached Chester Square and the safe haven of her own bedroom before the agony of what was undoubtedly the final parting from him actually hit her. And then she had to talk to Charles.

He was icily ruthless with her. He told her he would like her to leave as soon as possible, and that he hoped she wasn't nurturing any idea that she could take Flora and James with her. 'I shall fight you for custody if you try and get them. You can obviously visit them regularly, I won't stand in your way. I shall make you a generous allowance obviously, you won't starve, or be homeless. I don't want to be accused of parsimony. But I would prefer not to see you except on 47 occasions like the children's birthdays, when I hope we can be civilised for their sakes.'

'Oh don't worry, Charles,' said Nell. 'I've seen some very uncivilised behaviour over the past few years. I think I know how *not* to behave, at least.'

He looked as almost shocked and discomfited as Nick had.

He was, in absolute terms very generous. He bought her the lease on a small cottage she had found and fallen in love with in Battersea, made her an annual allowance which provided her with the bread and butter of life (although very little jam), and allowed her to have the children to stay for one weekend a month. Nell didn't contest any of this. She knew that she was in danger of being worse off (Charles having instant access to the finest legal advice in the country), and besides, she didn't have the heart.

1984

Sarah Jane Coleman was born at the West London Hospital with the absolute minimun of discomfort, and lay on her mother's breast looking up at her with eyes as large and velvety-dark as her father's. 'They're going to haunt me, those eyes,' said Nell tenderly.

'What was that, Mrs Coleman?' said the midwife.
'Nothing wrong, is there, she's beautiful.'

'No, nothing wrong,' said Nell, stroking the tiny nose, smiling at the waving frond-line fingers, love surging through her, sweetly, powerful. 'Nothing wrong at all.

Unless you can count looking just like her father.'

The midwife, who was very much from the new school, laughed.

Nell rather enjoyed her stay in hospital. She had been bored after the birth of Flora and James, lying alone in her flower-filled room at the London Clinic; she found the bustle of the public ward, hearing the life stories, watching the families pour in to meet their new members, enchanting.

Everyone was very nice to her; she was in a majority in the ward in having no husband, although most people had far more visitors. A few loyal friends popped in once or twice, although most of their cicle had inevitably sided with Charles; Mary Harris, her next-door neighbour from Battersea, who had befriended her and had called the ambulance for her, came nearly every day, bearing clean nightdresses and gossip (and was sent out each time for smoking in the ward), and so did Nell's new friend, Melanie Jeffries. Melanie was a solicitor and had acted for her over the purchase of her house; she had been driven to despair by Nell's passive attitude, had wanted her to fight Charles for more maintenance, but they had become very close despite Nell's refusal, and spent long giggly evenings in Nell's small front room plotting the downfall of men in general and the two in Nell's life and the one in Melanie's in particular.

Sarah Jane was a very good baby. She took her duties seriously and slept, ate and grew with admirable efficiency; Nell, struggling against loneliness and a financial situation that was challenging, if not exactly hard, added gratitude to the other more conventional maternal emotions. The days were all right; she cared for the baby, shopped and cooked and cleaned her little house. But the evenings were endlessly silent and solitary, apart from the one or two a week she spent with Melanie. Sometimes she could pass twenty-four hours without exchanging a single word with anyone.

She very seldom saw Charles, communicating with him almost entirely through his secretary and the nanny; Nick Buitoni wrote occasional letters, and sent her a huge bouquet of flowers when Sarah Jane was born. Nell sent them back and ignored his letters, but she was shocked to find how much she missed him still. The initial hurt had healed but the scars were still horribly fresh: fresh enough to send her into paroxysms of grief when she read a story in the *Daily Mail* about him and his new live-in lover, described by the *Daily Mail* as 'lovely, leggy society beauty Candida Curtis', who had heard his cabaret at the Savoy and fallen head over heels in love with him.

'The nearest she's been to society is when her gran joined the Co-op,' said Melanie tartly. 'Nell darling, don't, don't cry so much, he's a filthy, faithless jerk, and hopefully Candida will make him very unhappy. Did you know about that song, incidentally?'

'What song?' said Nell, turning a ravaged face back to Melanie.

'It says here he wrote a song a year or two back which he does in cabaret called – let me see – "Cinderella", and it's just won some award or other and –'

'Oh yes,' said Nell, very quietly, 'yes, I know about that song.'

And the memory of standing there, listening to Nick playing it on his old piano, reciting the terrible words, smiling at her, hurt so much, was so fierce, she thought she was actually going to faint. It went on all summer, the song, playing endlessly, haunting her, actually reaching the Number Twelve slot before finally fading into the obscurity she longed for.

'I think you should do something with your life,' said Melanie as Sarah Jane slept in her determined way and they munched pizzas and half watched a terrible miniseries on television. 'You're much too bright to sit around being a kept woman. Didn't you ever think of training at something?'

'No,' said Nell humbly. 'I never did. I just met bloody Prince Charming and got married.'

'Well it's never too late. Look at you, you're lonely and you're bored, it's a terrible waste. Does anything appeal to you?'

Nell thought for a bit. Then: 'Yes,' she said, surprising even herself. 'What you do appeals to me a lot.'

She wrote (after much prompting from Melanie, shortly after Sarah Jane's first birthday) to London University, asked them about the possibility of reading law as a mature student; to her astonishment they told her she had the necessary A levels. Charles was plainly and interestingly furious when she told him. She enrolled at King's College, London in October of 1985, nervous, fearful of failure, protesting that she would not be able to cope with the work, that Sarah Jane would suffer; but Melanie drove her on, 51 alternately bullying and encouraging her, and Mary Harris said she would look after Sarah Jane while she was in lectures, promising on her grandmother's grave not to smoke while she did so. Nell had a feeling that the grandmother's grave might have turned a few times, but on the whole Mary clearly made an enormous effort.

Charles refused to give Nell any more money, so she sold her rather battered old Renault 5 to pay Mary. Melanie was beside herself with rage, and wanted to take Charles to court, but Nell said she couldn't afford to run the car anyway, it was nothing but a liability and she'd decided to get a bicycle instead. She cycled up to the Strand whenever the weather was half nice enough, and as soon as Sarah Jane was old enough, she got a little seat for her on the back at weekends. Sarah Jane loved it, and when James and Flora came to visit, James brought his own bike, greatly to his father's irritation, and they cycled round Battersea Park together, but Flora, who was by now a slightly sanctimonious eight-year-old, said it was very dangerous and waited for them in Mary's house until they got back. There was a phone call from Charles next day to say if Nell was going to leave the children unsupervised, their visits would have to cease.

Nell loved the course; she had the kind of carefully enquiring and retentive mind that was entirely appropriate to the law, and even the areas she had expected find dry and possibly dull she discovered to be wonderfully engaging. Her essays after a rather faltering start were thoughtful as well as thorough, original as well as sound; her confidence grew, she laughed more, worried less, and realised with surprise as her first year neared its end that she had hardly thought about Nick Buitoni for weeks, and then with a kind of cheerful contempt.

'Told you,' said Melanie when she graduated. 'I'm beginning to wish I'd never encouraged this. I'll have to look out when you finally hit the firms.'

'Don't be silly,' said Nell, 'I only got a Two Two.'

'Bloody impressive, with a baby to look after, and a mean pig of a husband who doesn't give you enough money for even a week's holiday. Honestly Nell, I just don't understand why you don't –'

'Melanie, I treated him very badly,' said Nell briefly, 'that's why I don't.'

'He treated you badly.'

'No he didn't. Not by his lights. And I don't want any more of his beastly money than I have to. The minute I really qualify, I'm not going to take another farthing from him.'

'You're mad,' said Melanie fondly.

SPRING 1994

'Eleanor, are you free? I'd like to talk to you about a new client.'

'Yes, of course,' said Eleanor, smiling carefully at David Bruce with what she hoped was the right mixture of professional cool and personal warmth. Davis was not only her immediate boss and mentor, he was very sexy in a rather serious way, divorced, plainly lonely, and engaging her sensibilities to a rather alarming degree. 'Give me ten minutes and I'll be in.'

'Good. It's a very interesting case. I think it would suit you.'

She had become Eleanor when she had been applying for her articles; it seemed more appropriate, more grown up than Nell. She liked being Eleanor, she felt for the first time in her life that she was a person she could respect. She had worked for Bruce Lowe Higgins for four years; four happy, absorbing years, and had just been made, to her immense pride, a junior, albeit salaried partner. She still lived in the little house in Battersea, rather more expensively decorated these days; and she had even bought herself a car, although she still cycled to work occasionally when the morning looked promising enough. Sarah Jane was at a state school in Battersea; she was funny, charming and extremely pretty, with what Eleanor perceived as a distressing musical talent. She played the piano and the saxophone with great skill, and sang beautifully; she was also a wonderful mimic. Sarah Jane being Melanie berating the male race, or Mary fanatically hiding a lit cigarette, made Eleanor weep with laughter.

James adored her, and loved the time he spent at the little house; but Flora, to her mother's grief, hated Sarah Jane and was slowly becoming estranged from them all.

She scarcely saw Charles; she was forced to see quite a lot about Nick Buitoni in the papers. He had become famous, as much for the string of pretty girls on his arm at first nights as for the three successful musicals he had now written. It enraged Eleanor that these items still has the power to wound her.

Bruce's, as it was known in the legal fraternity, was a small young City firm, fast gaining a reputation for its skill in the libel area; Eleanor had worked successfully on several cases now, the most recent being against a women's magazine that had managed to imply in the most simpering adulatory copy that her client, a young actress, was not only a alcoholic, but extremely stupid with it. It had brought her some notoriety, and she had been interviewed with her client on a morning television programme and said absolutely nothing while appearing to say a great deal.

'Well now,' said David Bruce, 'let me tell you about this case. It's basically about plagiarism. Funny chap, name of Richardson, says he wrote a song that's been stolen from him. Years ago, apparently, and he'd given up any hope of getting any satisfaction, tried a couple of times, but he met our friend Archie Tremain QC at a party, who told him he really ought to go for it, told him he'd act for him even. I suppose he thought it would be fun; there'll be a lot of publicity, I would think.'

'Goodness,' said Eleanor. 'It sounds very intriguing. There must be a lot at stake. What's the song?'

'Never heard of it myself,' said David Bruce, 'but my secretary had. One of these Lloyd-Webber type numbers. It's called "Cinderella".'

Jack Richardson was a shabbily good-looking man in his

early thirties, with only shadows of the handsome boy who had dreamed of being a star. He had, he told Eleanor, been working as a video salesman for the past five years.

'You left showbiz, then?'

'Yes, in despair. I knocked around the business, auditioned endlessly, never got anything, you can't imagine how tough it is –'

'I think I can,' said Eleanor. 'Actually. Now let's begin at the beginning, shall we?'

Jack Richardson had written the song, he said, for an audition for a cabaret slot on one of the big liners. 'I thought it might help, if I did something original.' It hadn't. He couldn't remember the date of the audition, only that it was some time in the spring of '83, 'at some terrible rehearsal room in South London, now a supermarket. Who'd have a record of that? How could I possibly find anyone else who was there, who might remember?' Richardson's agent at the time was little use as a witness, 'drunk himself to death.'

Nick Buitoni had been at the audition too, had heard Richardson sing; they'd chatted briefly. Now he denied ever being there, said he'd been in the States at the time. His agent confirmed it. Eighteen months later, when Cinderella had its surprise hit, Richardson had written to him and told him the song was his. Buitoni had ignored his letter. 'Of course I didn't have much written down, just meaningless scribbles, and he'd obviously changed bits here and there. Who'd believe that?'

'I would,' said Eleanor.

*

'This whole thing,' said David Bruce with a sigh, as they discussed it late one night, 'hangs not just on Richardson being able to prove Buitoni heard the bloody song, but that he was actually at the audition at all. All those years ago. It looks impossible.'

'Nothing's impossible,' said Eleanor.

The case became a *cause célèbre*, it caught the public fancy. The various witnesses were theatre in themselves. Buitoni was impressive; charming, relaxed, slightly amused. Why should he stoop to such a thing? He was hugely successful in his own right, had already had his first hit 'Wintersong' (albeit slightly more modest) when 'Cinderella' came out; it was ridiculous. He might have met Richardson, who could possibly recall every crossed path in twenty years in showbusiness, but he certainly didn't remember him. The jury nodded knowingly, as if they spent much of their time in auditions. Buitoni's agent was sincerity itself, an English gentleman to his well-kept fingertips. ('Oh for a Flash Harry!' groaned Eleanor when she first saw him.) Of course Mr Buitoni had written the song himself; he could remember him coming in, slightly apologetically, with an early draft, he had sung the now-famous words to him across the desk, and they had both laughed, then agreed they had a potential hit.

Richardson was nervous, pale; he sounded whingeing. It was the word of one man against the other. Public sympathy was firmly behind the hero, behind Prince Charming as the tabloids called him.

*

Eleanor was unprepared for her emotions when she first saw Nick Buitoni in court. She had expected to feel tough and distant and cool; she felt instead frail and involved and shaken. She wondered what she could be doing, why she had ever agreed to take him on. Memories of love, long buried, surfaced painfully, agonisingly. Against every odd, she did not want to be the one who defeated him. And then one day as she walked out of the law courts, down the Strand, he confronted her, half smiling, half rueful, totally confident she would want to talk to him.

'I can't believe you're doing this,' he said, 'after everything we had.'

'I can,' she said. 'After everything you had.'

Suddenly the case turned. Archie Tremain QC, acting for Jack Richardson, said he would like to call Miss Patrice Prentice.

Patrice Prentice was an ex-Tiller girl. She had been at the audition, she remembered it because she had been successful, got a season on the liner. She also remember Buitoni well, because she had rushed in late and he had been kind to her, helped her get out her music, held her wrap while she danced.

'And Mr Richardson, do you remember him?'

'Yes, because they told him to wait, then they changed their minds. He was very dejected.'

'Do you remember the song?'

'No, I'm afraid I don't. Not really. I'm sorry.'

'Thank you Miss Prentice. You've been very helpful
indeed.'

It wasn't exactly conclusive, but it was impressive; it made Buitoni appear considerably less reliable as a witness. Archie Tremain made much of it in his final speech; the judge referred to it in his summing up.

The jury had been out for seven hours when they finally brought in their verdict that Nick Buitoni was guilty of plagiarism; Richardson was awarded a quarter of a million pounds with costs.

Later, much later, after much champagne had been drunk at the Savoy, and Jack Richardson had finally departed with his new agent to discuss contracts, David Bruce took Eleanor out to dinner and told her he'd like to buy her a great many more if she'd let him. She said not unless she was allowed to buy him an equal number: 'I'm an independent creature, David, you have to understand that.'

'Well so long as you'll be independent alongside me, I think I can handle it.'

'Good,' said Eleanor, smiling at him, feeling happiness filling her, warming her.

'Good case,' he said, raising a glass to her. 'Well done. Marvellous, the way you unearthed Ms Prentice like that. I still can't imagine how you knew she was there that day.'

'Oh,' said Eleanor thoughtfully, thinking of the yellowing scrap of paper she had never quite been able to throw away, that was a running order for an audition, with the first terrible words of Cinderella scribbled on the back. 'Just think of it as a variation on the glass slipper story. And this one fitted rather well.'

A Note on Penny Vincenzi

Penny Vincenzi began her career as a junior secretary for *Vogue* magazine and *Tatler*. She later worked as Fashion and Beauty Editor on magazines such as *Woman's Own*, *Nova* and *Honey*, before becoming a Deputy Editor for *Options*, and contributing Editor for *Cosmopolitan*. She is the author of two humorous books, and five novels, *Old Sins*, *Wicked Pleasures*, *An Outrageous Affair*, *Another Woman* and *Forbidden Places*. Her sixth novel is due to be published by Orion in 1996. Penny Vincenzi is married with four daughters.